To my brave chicks, Allen, Steven, and Jaimie

—L. M.

For Hana, Marnie, Teresa, Sally, and Rachel,
who are all very good eggs

—N. V. C.

Henry Holt and Company, LLC, *Publishers since 1866*
175 Fifth Avenue, New York, New York 10010 • mackids.com

Henry Holt® is a registered trademark of Henry Holt and Company, LLC.
Text copyright © 2016 by Lori Mortensen
Illustrations copyright © 2016 by Nina Victor Crittenden
All rights reserved.

Library of Congress Cataloging-in-Publication Data
Mortensen, Lori, date.
Chicken Lily / Lori Mortensen ; illustrated by Nina Victor Crittenden. — First edition.
pages   cm
Summary: "Through puns and poetry, Chicken Lily overcomes her fears and reads a poem onstage at her school poetry jam" —Provided by publisher.
ISBN 978-1-62779-120-5 (hardback)
[1. Fear—Fiction. 2. Poetry slams—Fiction. 3. Chickens—Fiction. 4. Domestic animals—Fiction.] I. Crittenden, Nina Victor, illustrator. II. Title.
PZ7.M84643Ch 2016   [E]—dc23   2015003263

Our books may be purchased in bulk for promotional, educational, or business use.
Please contact your local bookseller or the Macmillan Corporate and Premium Sales Department at
(800) 221-7945 ext. 5442 or by e-mail at MacmillanSpecialMarkets@macmillan.com.

First Edition—2016 / Book designed by Anna Booth
The art for this book was created with watercolor, pen, and ink on Arches hot pressed watercolor paper.
Printed in China by Toppan Leefung Printing Ltd., Dongguan City, Guangdong Province

1 3 5 7 9 10 8 6 4 2

CHICKEN LILY

Lori Mortensen

ILLUSTRATED BY Nina Victor Crittenden

Henry Holt and Company

NEW YORK

Lily was a lot of things:

a careful colorer,

a patient puzzler,

and the quietest hide-and-seeker.
She never made a peep!

But Lily was also something else . . .

Chicken.

While her friends zoomed around on their bikes,
Lily rode with training wheels. *Clunk, rattle, rattle.*
Clunk, rattle, rattle.

"Look! No hooves!" shouted Pigsley.

"When are you going to take off your training wheels, Lily?" asked Baabette.

"Someday," said Lily. But she wished she could keep them on forever.

At school, Lily never raised her wing, even when she knew the answer.

"Why did the chicken cross the road?" asked her teacher, Mrs. Lop.

Paws shot up all around the room.

"To go to the store?"

"To play at the park?"

"Because it was time to go home?"

To get to the other side, thought Lily.

But Lily didn't make a peep.

At lunch, Lily turned up her beak no matter what was served.

"Haystacks?"

"Sloppy joes?"

"Shepherd's pie?"

Lily shook her head and pecked at her sack of chicken feed.

"You're just chicken," said Baabette.

"What if it tastes yucky?" said Lily.

"What if it tastes good?"

Lily wasn't taking any chances.

The next day,
Mrs. Lop posted
a big notice on the
bulletin board.

MRS. LOP'S CLASS

GRAND-SLAM POETRY JAM

DO YOU LIKE TO WRITE IN RHYME?

WANT TO HAVE A REAL GOOD TIME?

GRAB YOUR PEN AND WRITE, WRITE, WRITE.

READ YOUR POEM TOMORROW NIGHT.

"I can't wait!" bleated Baabette.

"Me neither!" squealed Pigsley.

"I can wait," Lily clucked to herself. Just thinking about reciting a poem *in front of everyone* sent shivers down her tail feathers.

Lily brooded about it the rest of the day. She couldn't help thinking of all the things that might go wrong. What if she sounded like a complete birdbrain?

BAWK
BAWK
BAWK

What if she fell flat on her beak?

What if she laid an egg?

That night, Lily hatched a plan.

She grabbed a pencil and wrote very carefully.

The next day, Lily unfurled a long list in front of her teacher.

"I *can't* be in the poetry jam, Mrs. Lop," said Lily.

"I've got too much to do."

Lily held her breath hopefully. There was no way she'd have to be in the Grand-Slam Poetry Jam now.

But to her surprise, Mrs. Lop held up her list like a gem.

"Look at this fine handwriting," exclaimed Mrs. Lop. "Anyone who writes this well *must* be in the poetry jam."

Lily

° Feather my nest.

° Put all my eggs in one basket.

° Count the chickens before they hatch.

Lily nearly molted.

"You're just chicken," said Baabette.

Lily didn't want to think about it.

But *not* thinking about it was impossible.

At lunch, Pigsley joked, "Broccoli looks just like trees. Maybe I'll write a poem about that."

At recess, Baabette clapped and sang, "Pat-a-cake, pat-a-cake, baker's man. Make me a poem as fast as you can!"

Posters were everywhere.

After school, Lily went home and tied red ribbons around her coop to make it a poem-free zone.

But her friends only wrote *more* poems.

"Stop being silly," said Baabette. "The poetry jam is tonight. You have to have a poem."

"No, I don't," said Lily stubbornly. She shut her eyes and covered her ears. When she opened her eyes . . .

. . . everyone was gone.

Lily felt like a rotten egg.

Deep down, she knew Baabette was right.

The only thing worse than reading a poem

would be standing onstage with *no* poem at all.

So Lily began to write.
Just a little.
One letter, then another.
A, B, C, D, E, F, G...

Lily decided that writing a poem was sort of like
putting together a puzzle.
Lily was good at puzzles.
When she finished, the only question was—
would she, could she, read it in front of everyone?

That night, Lily crowded onto the stage
with the rest of her class.

One by one, Lily's friends got up
and read their poems.

"*Broccoli is my favorite food.*
I like it best with cheese.
But what I really like the most
Is how it looks like trees!"

Then it was Lily's turn.
She wished she could fly
the coop. As she walked to
the microphone, the audience
smiled and clapped.
Her friends did too.

Lily could and would
read her poem.

"*A, B, C, D, E, F, G . . .*
Writing poems is fun for me.
When we're done and out the door,
I'll go home and write some more!"

Lily was a lot of things:

a careful colorer,

a patient puzzler,

and the quietest hide-and-seeker.
(She never made a peep.)

But Lily was also something else . . .

Chicken.

Just not all the time.

Mrs. Lop

Baabette

Jay

Pigsley

Drake

Bonnie